FACES

written by **SHELLEY ROTNER** and **KEN KREISLER**

photographs by **SHELLEY ROTNER**

MACMILLAN PUBLISHING COMPANY • NEW YORK

MAXWELL MACMILLAN CANADA • TORONTO

MAXWELL MACMILLAN INTERNATIONAL
NEW YORK • OXFORD • SINGAPORE • SYDNEY

Macmillan Publishing Company is part of the
Maxwell Communication Group of Companies.
Macmillan Publishing Company
866 Third Avenue
New York, NY 10022
Maxwell Macmillan Canada, Inc.
1200 Eglinton Avenue East
Suite 200
Don Mills, Ontario M3C 3N1
First edition
Printed in Hong Kong

10 9 8 7 6 5 4 3 2 1

The text of this book is set in 24 point Memphis Medium.

Library of Congress Cataloging-in-Publication Data

Rotner, Shelley.
Faces / by Shelley Rotner and Ken Kreisler ; photos by
Shelley Rotner. — 1st ed.   p.   cm.
Summary: A photographic concept book that emphasizes
the things all people have in common, rather than
the things that keep us apart.
ISBN 0-02-777887-8
1. Face perception—Juvenile literature.   2. Similarity
(Psychology)—Juvenile literature.   [1. Face.   2. Similarity
(Psychology)   3. Individuality.]   I. Kreisler, Ken.
II. Rotner, Shelley, ill.   III. Title.
BF242.R67   1994   153.7′5—dc20   93-46758

In memory of my grandmother—
a face I will always remember.
—S. R.

For Samantha
—K. K.

Faces, faces, all kinds of faces.

Faces talking,

faces smelling,

faces hearing,

faces seeing.

Thinking faces,

sleeping faces,

friendly faces,

faces feeling.

Funny faces

sometimes masked,

sometimes painted.

All different,

each special in its own way.

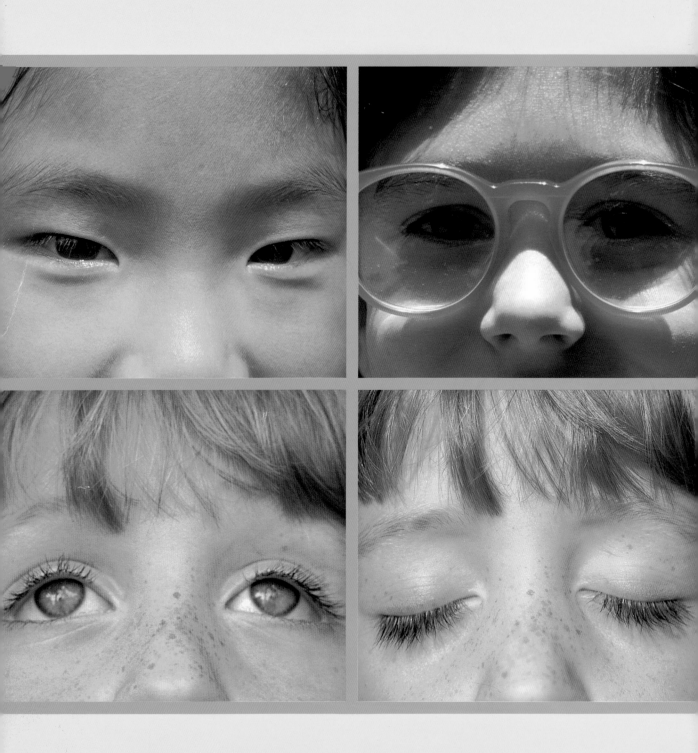

Eyes,

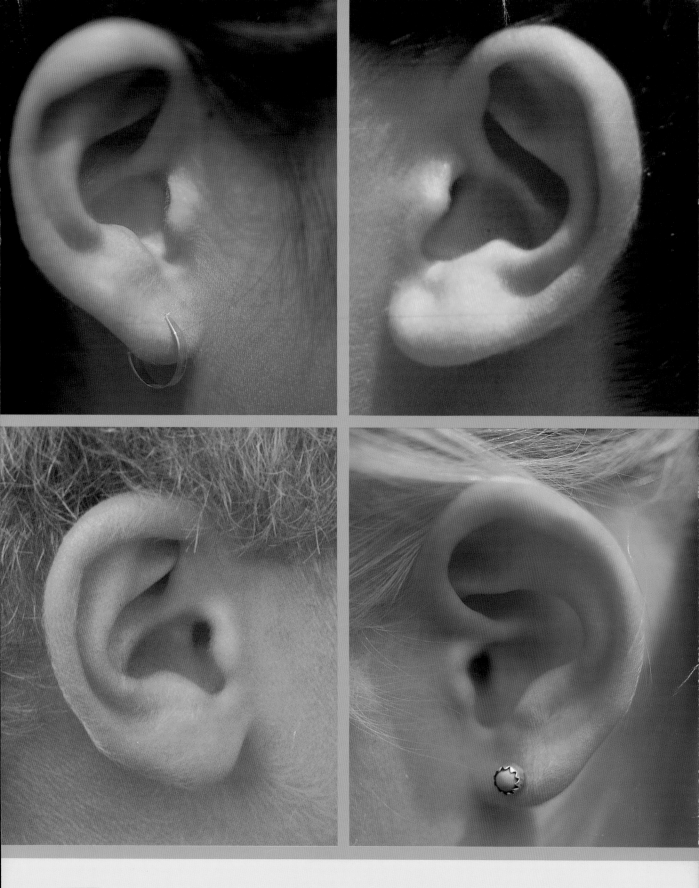

ears.

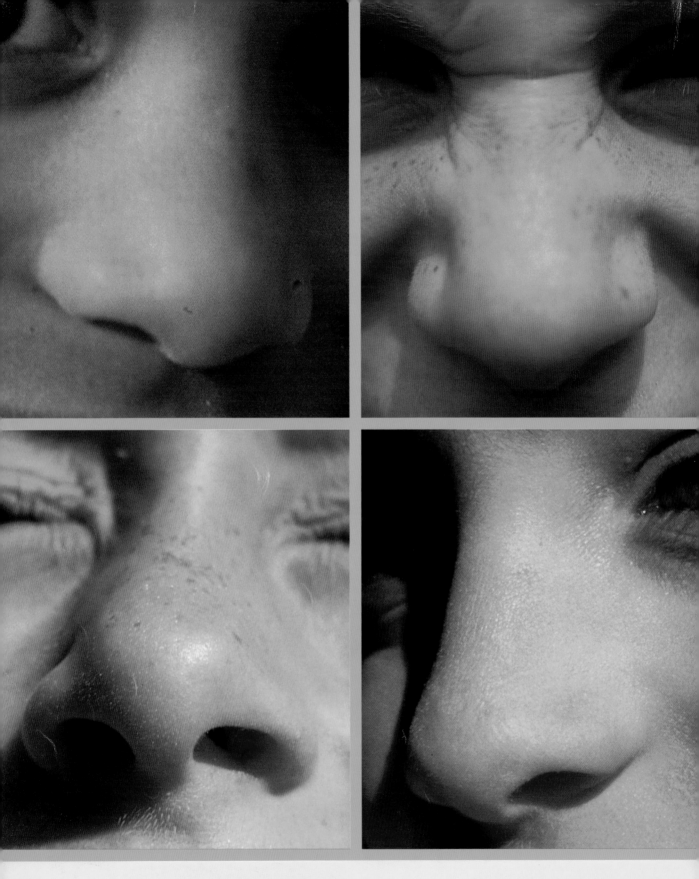

Noses,

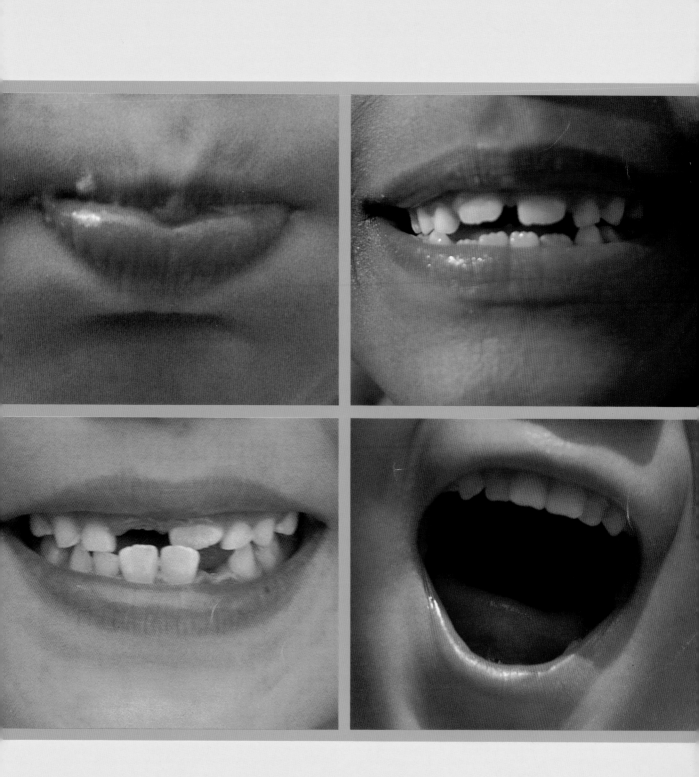

mouths.

Faces, faces, from all kinds of places.

Faces.